Tangled Shadows

Tangled Shadows

I wrote this book when I was twenty to twenty-three, between 2011-2014. I saw someone reading "50 Shades of Grey" on the L (train), and I said to myself "that's what I will do, write about my sex life, and make millions of dollars". I did not make millions of dollars, yet, and I regret writing about sex. I was going to, and still kind of want to, black out the sexual content in this edition, but I think it would lower the quality of the novel. Maureen Dezell in her book "Irish America: Coming Into Clover", quoting Rev. Liam Ryan writes, "One of the deadly sins of Irish Catholicism: an obsession with sexual morality" page 183 (which I think is a good thing).

I wanted to be like Norman Mailer: invited on all the T.V. shows, to all the parties, and have an upperclass East Coast WASP wife. What a pretentious dilettante I was.

I was trying to write something both hyper modern, and eternal.

I wrote a very good novel. I will let others decide if it is a great novel.

Now, I am trying to finish my second novel, "The Depth of Middleclass Sorrow: a comedy".

Tangled Shadows

Blue sunlight glows through white plastic blinds onto the stucco walls of my apartment. I sit lotus on tan fuzz-carpet. The milky blue light mutates to orange and lemon jam as the sun rises.

I am looking out the window when I get a text from Amanda.

"Want 2 fuck?"

"My place or yours?" I text back.

"Urs"

"Bring some weed"

"K"

I don't like Amanda in a romantic way. She is one of those people obsessed with drugs and I could never be as important to her as her next line. I met her at a party and we had sex in the overcast morning of the next day.

I step out of the shower, grab a towel, dry off, shave, and brush my teeth.

Amanda texts me again.

"5 min"

I get dressed and walk to the train station. The train pulls in. About six people get off. Amanda walks down the ramp. I wait for her. She steps in front of me. I bend down and we kiss. Holding hands we walk back to my apartment.

I shut my apartment door behind us. Making out I rub her labia and clit through her pants. Bite-kiss-sucking her neck. She unhooks her bra from under her shirt and strips. I take off my clothes. Walking a few steps back she sits on the couch. I follow on my knees. I lick her wet delicious pussy. She grabs the top of my hair, pulls my head up, and kisses me. I balance myself on my right knee and dig inside her. She moans. My arms stroke the soft skin of her legs. The short hairs of her pelvis scratch the inside of my thighs. I look at the black ink swan on her hip. I come on her stomach. She dips her fingers in some and tastes it. She grins. I get up, give her a paper towel, walk over to the fridge, and get two beers. We throw our twist tops in unison into the kitchen near the trash. She gets a cigarette cellophane wrapper, melted at the top, with pot inside, from her purse. I open it with my thumbs and middle fingers like a fortune cookie. Looking at it in my left palm the evergreen bud has maroon strands and big white crystals. She gets my red bowl with white stripes from my dresser. I grind the marijuana in my palm. Then I cover the hole at the bottom of the pipe with a small nug and fill it with fine weed. In yesterday's jeans I find my black disposable lighter with the child safety removed.

I finish my beer and put it on the table at the end of the couch. She leaves hers a quarter-full on the carpet.

We get dressed. She lays her bra on the arm of the couch. I don't put on my socks.

I walk over to the sliding glass door, open it, walk onto the porch followed by her, and close it behind us. We sit on two grey plastic lawn chairs facing south. I let her take greens and I have Tuesdays. The smoke drifts over strips of grass stretching between the sidewalks and the street, telephone wires, brick two flats, people, and cars.

My body is warm and I become aware of my thoughts.

Things are composed of chemicals and geometric forms adhering to laws that are exact throughout the universe and wisdom is the highest achievement.

Amanda brings her legs to her body and holds them. I turn to her.

Me: The irony of the media is they claim to be independent but they depend on the status quo of Washington politics and capitalist economics.

Amanda: Mmhmm.

I thought it was a good comment. Maybe I'm wrong.

One of my neighbors is walking below. I hide the spoon in my hand pressing it against my shirt and stomach. He gets into his car and drives away. I put my feet on the metal porch railing, and take another hit, then pass it to Amanda. She packs the weed down with the bottom corner of the lighter.

It feels like there is something I know. But what is it? It is on the tip of my tongue. Now it is off in the distance annoying me.

She cashes the pipe, then we go inside, and have intercourse on the floor.

We stare at the ceiling. Her head is on my right shoulder. Hair brushing my skin.

Amanda: Do you want to get some wine?

I go into the liquor store through automatic doors. The entrance is a hallway of promotional cardboard boxes filled with liquor bottles.

I imagine tripping on a box knocking it down in a loud crash. A sales clerk gives me an angry look because they will have to clean it up. The manager who tries to avoid all negative confrontation will put his hands up, asking if I am all right, and tell me not to worry, then call over some unfortunate to take care of this mess. I'll mumble a convincing but insincere apology. Maybe not so convincing. The rum will turn into a small brown lake with yellow caution signs indicating the local site of broken glass. I'll get my wine and leave with a smile.

There is a sale on a gallon of vodka for twelve dollars. I resist the impulse to buy everything in the store that has good market value. I grab a Shiraz from Chile and get in line behind an old bald white man buying a gallon of vodka.

The young cashier asks for my ID. She smiles at me and types my birthdate into the computer. I nod.

At my place I get two large water glasses and fill them with wine. I take a sip. It's pretty good for six dollar wine. I drink it slowly like coffee.

I become engulfed in a warm inebriation. I pour another huge glass of rouge liquid for myself. I meet eyes with Amanda, give a drunken smile, roll my eyes, and slump in my chair. The sweet wine hangs in my mouth even once it's in my stomach. I grab Amanda's hand, take her to my bed, and wrap myself around her.

I'm on a city street naked. It is desolate and the lights are blurry blueish yellow.

At a hospital I'm staring in a full-length mirror. I see something demonic behind me.

I wake up terrified. I don't remember what happened then the horrible image burns in my mind. I get out of bed and walk into the living room. I go back to my room and lie beside Amanda. It's dark except for a white line shining on my wall and ceiling. I turn on my side and put a pillow over my head.

I wake the next afternoon and Amanda is gone. About thirty percent of the wine is left. The cork is at an angle. No missed calls or received texts. From my medicine cabinet I get a vitamin B and drink it with a glass of water.

*

I walk into a cafe across the street from my apartment and order a large coffee. Cafes are modern opium dens for suburban housewives and IT guys. The cashier pours my coffee from a pull down tap behind him and hands it to me. I add some cream at the milk cart then sit down at a round table.
Customers recite complicated orders like their social security numbers.
I drink a quarter of my coffee. The caffeine flows through my veins filling my mind with ecstasy. It feels exactly like cocaine without the need to listen to funk or lick mirrors. I pick up a newspaper from the table next to me.
"Yesterday morning an unidentified body was found behind a shopping center in Schaumburg. The throat was cut open, which was ruled to be the cause of death, and the body had been disfigured. The victim was a middle-age male, six feet and approximately 175 pounds. There are currently no suspects. The Schaumburg police ask, if you

have any information about the incident, to please contact them."

I put the paper down. Tragedies every day.

I finish my coffee then leave. I walk towards the street and stand on the curb with my toes over the edge. I step back before a car goes by in the lane closest to me.

Across this street and in front of my building is a brick strip mall. There is a business in the mall that I am not sure what it does. It could be a for-profit charity or a pyramid scheme. There are always groups of people standing around holding plastic binders.

Once I have gotten home safely and locked my door I often feel I have narrowly escaped being murdered by an unknown person. Rarely do I feel once I leave my house I am going to be killed.

I take off my shoes and check my phone. Nothing. I pace the living room, to the bedroom, back to the living room. Sit down. Get up. Sit down. Get up. Walk backwards, then forwards, and backwards, and forwards. Open the sliding glass door, walk out, and stand on the porch then go back inside. I put my face against the glass.

Me: Uhhh.

The clock ticks religiously.

Should I go for a walk? I put on my shoes and grab my keys.

It is warm and dark outside. Cream clouds are stuck in the chocolate sky. Dry leaves smell like youth's wisdom; colors of acorn, spiced rum, plum, beets, ash, gold. A bush makes a sound like a rattlesnake when the wind rustles its leaves. Cicadas hum and crickets yell hidden in the shadows.

I wish Amanda was here.

I walked twenty-three blocks west. The only other people I saw were walking tethered canines or operating automobiles. When I was two blocks from my apartment it began to drizzle.

I turn in bed for a while listening to the rain tap the window before I fall asleep.

I am walking around my living room when I get a call from my Uncle Bob.

Bob: Alex! Would you like to work?

Me: Yeah.

Bob: Then come to the office now!

Bob has a small office that does administrative contract jobs for larger companies.

I get my car keys and walk down the grey cement stairwell at the end of the hall.

I drive past potholes swamped with rainwater and dead leaves.

In the office parking lot a tree's leaves silhouette on Bob's red car. I walk into the basement. Grey concrete walls and steel beam rafters surround the office. Fluorescent lights on the ceiling. Bob is standing behind his solid wood desk on the phone.

Bob: I can get it to you Thursday - I have to go - okay, okay - bye.

He hangs up the phone and stares at me.

Bob (Moving his hands like a symphony conductor): Alex buddy! Are you ready to work?

Me: Sure.

Bob: Okay. I need you to do last month's Nash Realty reports.

He grabs a file crate with Nash Realty's sales reports from the silver file cabinet and puts it on my greenish-grey metal desk. I move it to my left, find an empty crate, and place it on the ground to my right. The computer is mismatched a beige tower and black monitor.

I open a spreadsheet and fill out the top columns with "Names, Amount, Paid, Total Due." Bob sits down at his desk and starts to write something. I feel like Sisyphus typing names and numbers that never end. The spreadsheet is morphing into a de Kooning painting and Rorschach blotter. I turn into a zombie transferring the information. I have no consciousness other than Mathew Schiff 426 Central Street $252,000 all paid.

Bob: How's it going?
Me: Fine. Maybe twenty more minutes.
I finish typing the report. My brain hurts.
Bob gives me two new vibrant crisp twenties.

*

I sit on my worn couch. The clean white plastic refrigerator with grey handles that has a twelve pack of Lite Beer with Lime (five left), bacon, orange juice, and hot sauce, hums.

I press the button for the elevator. It clunks and whooshes up. The metal door slides behind the wall. The elevator is empty. I get in. It buzzes down two floors and bounces on the ground level. I step onto the brown carpet, take a right, look at the yellow wallpaper, and open the green metal door with white words that say "Storage Locker." It is a room full of small wire cages. It resembles a cramped cellblock for excess possessions. I turn on the overhead sixty-watt row of mine-like lights. My bicycle stands on its back wheel leaning against its left handle on the far wall. I unlock a silver padlock the size of an infant's fist with a small golden key. I roll the blue antique out of the cage, close the lock with my free left hand, and pull it out backwards to the lobby. I swing the front glass door open and pull my bike through to outside. I ride past five blocks of apartments, two convenience stores, a gas station, an erotica store, a few restaurants, a hotel, and a grade school. When I let go of my pedals they slowly turn like a Ferris wheel.

The grocery store is a giant tan building maybe the size of two-and-a-half football fields with an even bigger parking lot. In front blue sedans and black SUVs dash around a snaked curved street.

Shopping carts are scattered in front of the complex. An employee shoves them inside each other consuming one another with their inverted metal tongues. The cheap plastic wheels rattle around the axles shaking the metal baskets. Like a fisherman securing the haul on a deck he heaves twenty carts in at a time. He pushes them widely to the left. They scrape the ground and bend in the middle. Bouncing around they seem like they are going to snap and break at the corners but they are sturdy like a bridge in a storm. Exhausted he wipes his forehead with his hand.

The carts have a strange biotic nature. Maybe they are reincarnated stockbrokers doomed to a life of servitude. The metal cages are ribs that hold food but won't digest it. A kid pushes one with a running start, jumps on, and rides the back like a silver skateboard tank. A young woman uses hers as a stroller for her baby. An elderly lady substitutes one for her walker.

The big red underlined letters with the store's name are deceptive. They could be for a cheap sporting goods store.

Using a combination chain lock I perpendicularly secure my bike to the silver bike rack that is not fastened to the ground. I enter the foyer through a shaky glass automated door. Black mats have collected weeks' worth of rain and dirt. I grab a grey plastic basket near the entrance that was once an insurance salesman. The blue speckled custard floor stained by milk and smudged with soil dully reflects the giant lights above.

I have no list but go over what I need in my head. Pasta, tomato sauce, broccoli, cream, parmesan, bread, eggs, butter.

The huge freezers with big clear doors and bronze handles are like upright tombs towering over shoppers. When I grab a frozen broccoli package vapor spins and pours out of the cryogenic carrot casket. When I get the eggs I mourn all the chickens put in cages and systematically butchered for our consumption. I remember my vote is not important. Try to get over being human. When I get the pasta I forget about my guilt. I wonder how can we maintain a stable economic system when agriculture is a dynamic variable?

On my way to the bakery I decide to sample some wine from a small old man with thick white hair.

Wine Guy: What would you like?

Me: I'll try a red.

Wine Guy: Something dry?

Me: Sure.

He pours the deep rojo liquid into a small plastic taster that should be used for cough medicine. It has that dry quality all the winos discuss so much but it tastes like the grapes were never loved.

Me: No. Could I try something else?

He starts to throw away my cup.

Me: It's fine don't need a new one.

He looks at me under his nose and out one eye with contempt.

Wine Guy: How about a dessert wine?

I've never had dessert wine.

Me: All right.

He fills my soiled plastic container with crimson fluid. It's appallingly sweet and bitter like cranberries but slightly better.

Me: Could I try another?

He grabs one of those 750 ml bottles and fills my cup. I don't like it. I point to the remaining bottle of red.

Me: How about that one?

He mumbles something I can't understand.

Me: Could I try that last one?

Wine Guy (Croak yell): Only three it's not a bar!

Me: Sorry. I couldn't hear you.

No shit it's not a bar. Asshole. I walk away. Was that a good one? I won't find out.

I finish my shopping and get in the checkout line behind a woman with neon green sweatpants, a neon orange tank top, and black flip flops. She hands the wrinkled female cashier her discount card.

Cashier (Smoky rural accent): We aint use that no more.

Customer: Oh. When did that happen?

Cashier: Bout three weeks ago.

The cashier scans the double fudge weight-loss bars and soyrizo imitation sausage.

Cashier: Six twenty-five.
The woman slides her debit card, enters her pin, and presses the green button.

In a frying pan I cook three strips of bacon, until they are red but not crispy, and scramble two eggs with the bacon. I put the eggs and bacon on a piece of bread then hot sauce on top. I bring my plate to my cheap square mahogany composite-wood table and set it down. I pour myself a glass of juice and get a fork. I feel like saying grace but it's just Christian guilt. Chew. Ingest. Gaze fixed at the plate and table.

I scrape the last of the eggs into a pile and put on more hot sauce. After the last bite I push the plate away like I'm never going to eat again. I finish my juice then put the red-stained plate with bits of dried egg in the sink. I wash out the glass, fill it with water, take a sip, and set it on the counter. I turn my head upward then look down at the watch that's not on my wrist. I text Amanda.

"Do you want to hangout?"
"I have a boyfriend"
"Good for you" I text sarcastically.

Snowing.
Christmas. I am alone.

It's New Year's Eve so I am going out to a bar. I get on a train headed downtown. I get off at Fullerton. I decided I'm going to walk until I see a bar that intrigues me. I see a bar I know but have never been in. I keep walking in case there is something better. I turn around after a block, walk back to the bar, and sit at the center in front of the bar. It's a common-type place with a few TVs and a wooden bar top.

There are two bartenders. A shorter one with large breasts and a taller skinny one. Both blonde.

Short Bartender: What do you want to drink?

Me: Bud Lite.

She grabs a glass and pulls down the tap filling the glass with sweet golden liquid.

Short Bartender: Four dollars.

I hand her a twenty. She gives me change and I put a dollar on the bar. I take a sip. The taller bartender is talking to a group of four people sitting at the bar.

Large man with short brown hair: All I need is enough for food, gas, and cigarettes.

The tall bartender nods with her arms crossed.

Large man with short brown hair: Everything is so expensive in the city. It's thirty dollars for a case. A case!

She nods some more. I see now that it is two guys with two girls. I wonder if they hate their boyfriends. I don't care. It's better if they don't. Maybe they're just friends.

I take a sip of my beer. I stare at a bottle of clear rum for a while.

When I finish my beer the taller bartender walks over.

Tall Bartender: Are you looking forward to a fun night?

You sound like a prostitute.

Me: Maybe.

Tall Bartender: Where are you from?

Me: Skokie. The north suburbs.

Tall Bartender: Well. It should be a fun night. New Year's Eve in the city.

Me: Yeah.

Tall Bartender: Do you want anything else?

Me: Later. Thanks.

The TVs are muted on a local channel. A boy who once had a promising basketball career is now paraplegic. It seems like they are playing a positive spin.

11:00 P.M. the bar becomes packed. The shorter girl walks in front of me and smiles.

Me: Whisky and Coke.

She grabs a small glass, fills it with ice, whisky, then coke from the fountain.

Short Bartender: Five dollars.

I hand her a five. She puts it in the register. I take a sip. All the people are enjoying themselves talking and laughing.

I continue to look at the rum. On the TV the Time Square testicular disco ball drops. Everyone in the bar cheers. I order another beer.

The bartenders pour Champagne in plastic flutes for everyone. The digital clock strikes twelve.

Everyone screams (Except for me): Happy New Year!

I finish my beer and Champagne then leave.

It is as cold as a refrigerator outside and the snow is like insulation.

I put water in a pan then turn on the stove. I lean against the counter. Cabinets. Stove dials.

The pan forms small bubbles on the bottom. I get tea from a box in the cabinet and a mug. I put the tea in the mug and pour in the simmering water. I wait about three minutes. Then I take out the bag and set it on its laminated package. Steam silently slithers from the surface. The water turned ash. I grab the mug's ear and sit down at the dining table. I agitate it like a beaker, then blow at the water, making ripples. Foam gathers at the top. The steam has slowed.

    I am enjoying this tea now but should I allow my indulgence to be more important than others' lives? Yes. But there is still needless suffering. Babies breathe the pollution of generations before them. Masses in poverty. Civilians slaughtered in worthless wars. Homosexuals are attacked and murdered. Respectable citizens are imprisoned for smoking a joint. People are not allowed to live in the countries they want. Women do not earn as much money as men. Black Americans can't even walk down the street without being stopped and questioned by the police. Why do people tacitly participate in these atrocities? Why are people complacent in having two similar choices to vote for? Humans are selfish but we all have similar goals and needs. I want clean water so we should all have clean water. There is nothing wrong with being rich but those in the aristocracy exploit workers and have more than they could ever use. And it seems like no one cares. They all decide their lives based on what seems cool. I want to go into a crowded place and yell. But what would that change? Maybe it is hopeless. I can just eat one dollar chicken sandwiches and heat my apartment for fifty dollars a month.

*

    Maybe I should see a movie or buy something. I shower and get dressed. The bus pulls up. Its hydraulics hiss as it drops down like a low-rider. I put two dollars and seventy-five cents into the money slot. It is a new bus with clean blue and grey cushion seats.

New Meadow, an outdoor mall, is a maze carved out of glass storefronts. A walkway of muted yellow, purple, and grey bricks flow like a river and spin into flower designs around trees. Child statues stand in a fountain. Carved marble horse heads preside in the shadow of a diamond store. Mothers and their children move under awnings. Teenagers wander in groups turning around to talk while texting. Kiosks of sunglasses, lotions, and cellphone cases are guarded by twenty-something entrepreneurs.

I look at the box office time board. Nothing I want to see.

Inside a clothing store I look at sweaters. I see a girl Hailey I know from a restaurant I worked at last year. It seems like she is with a friend. I go up to them.

Me: Hello.

Hailey: Hey.

Me: What are you doing here?

Hailey: Just shopping with Isabella. This is Alex.

Hailey turns her right palm up indicating to me.

It seems as if months pass as I stare at Isabella's perfect Arabian brown eyes and shining black hair. She smiles. I nod stupidly.

Isabella: Hey.

Me: Nice to meet you.

Is there nothing better to say?

Me (To Hailey): So are you still working at The Sliced Kitchen?

Hailey: Yeah. It's the same old routine. Most people left and I'm thinking about leaving too.

Me: Oh. Well. We should hang out sometime.

Hailey: Yeah. Definitely.

Me: What's your number?

I take out my phone.

Hailey: Eight four.
Me: Here.
I hand her the phone. She types her number.
Me: Well. It was great to see you. I'll talk to you guys later.
Hailey: Yeah. You too.
Isabella: Bye.
Me: Bye.
I have no intention of buying anything so I leave.
I stare out the bus window. I am excited that I have even seen Isabella. I don't know why. I barely know her. There is a light in my life. A fire in my heart. Only death can upset me. I get off at the corner and sit against my living room wall. I text Hailey.
"Do you and Isabella want to come over tonight?"
I pour myself whisky and orange juice and sit back down against the wall.
"Sounds good" she replies.
"My address is 1491 elmwood, skokie. Let me know when youre here."
"K"
The liquor burns nicely through my veins.
Hailey texts me that they're here.
I go down the elevator. Isabella and Hailey are outside the entrance door. Isabella looks at me through the glass. Hailey is staring at the mailboxes. I open the door. Hailey turns.
Me: Hey.
Hailey: Hey.
They walk in.
Hailey: How's it going?
Me: It's fine. I'm just sitting around.

I press the button for the elevator.
We stand in the lift without talking or making eye contact.
I open my apartment door and take off my shoes.
Hailey: Do you want us to take our shoes off?
Me: No. It's fine. I just like to.
They both take off their shoes. Isabella is wearing long black socks.
Me: Do you want drinks?
Hailey: Yeah.
Isabella: Me too.
I make them drinks.
Hailey: Cheers.
We all clink cups.
Me: Cheers.
Isabella: Cheers.
We sit down.
Hailey: That's a nice mirror.
There is a large mirror hanging on my dining area wall. I find it unnecessary.
Me: It's my aunt's. This is her place but I stay here while she is gone.
Hailey: Where is she?
Me: Michigan.
Hailey is talking but I am not paying attention.
I finish my drink.
Hailey: Do you have any dessert?
Me: No. Sorry.
Hailey: Do you want to go to Celia's Cakes?
Me: Yeah. Sure.
I sit in the back of Hailey's white cop-like car. The grey leather sticks and smacks when touched. Her radio has bright green numbers. 8:43.

Celia's is a bakery of mostly single-serve orders. Light blasts through the store windows under the dark sky. The walls are burgundy. The menu is written in white chalk on a blackboard behind the counter. Bakery racks encrusted with dough wait in front of glowing red ovens. Muffins, cookies, brownies, scones, and other sweets are piled on the marble counter behind a glass shield. On top of white stands, like Roman columns, the cakes and pies are like flowers. Some with petals missing.

I am tempted to get a lemon bar but I fear I may regret it as a bad fiscal decision in the future. Hailey gets a chocolate chip cookie the size of one of those giant flat circle lollipops. We sit at a bench inside the store. Hailey breaks off a third of the cookie and hands it to Isabella.

Me: Could I try a bite?

Hailey hands me a piece. Buttery and salty. The chocolate is sweet.

Me: So. Do people call you Bella?
Isabella: People call me Bella but not Isabell.
Me: Izzy?
Isabella: Sometimes.
Hailey: I have to go to the bathroom.
Isabella: Do you want me to go with you?
Hailey: No. It's fine.
She puts her cookie down and gets up.
I can't think of anything meaningful to say.
Me: So. Do you go to school or work?
Isabella: I go to school.
Me: Where?
Isabella: East State.
Me: What are you studying?
Isabella: Neuroscience.

Me: Do you have a boyfriend?
She smiles.
Isabella: No. Do you have a girlfriend?
I smile.
Me: No. Can I get your number?
Isabella: Yeah.
She tells me her phone number.
Isabella: You can call or text me anytime.
Hailey comes back and finishes the cookie.
Hailey drives me home.
I sit around for twenty minutes trying to be nonchalant. Then I open my text messages, wait longer, trying to psychically push the seconds into minutes. I give up on time travel and type to Isabella
"I think I have a schoolboy crush on you."
and press send.
I wait in complete fear. What if what I said was stupid? I thought it was accurate. I look at the sent time. It's been two minutes.
"What are you going to do about it?"
I grin.
"Do you want to go to dinner and a movie tomorrow night?"
"Yes"
"Meet me in front of the evanston theater at 6?"
"Ok"
I'm fucking elated.
I make myself a drink and sit on my bed.

I am walking down the sidewalk. Isabella is in front of the cinemaplex. She does not notice me until I am about four feet from her.

Me: Hey.

Isabella (Whimsically): Hey.

Me: I thought we could see The Lonesome Circle.

Isabella: That's what I was thinking.

It's about a cowboy's struggle with love and alcohol.

A gargantuan serpentine moving staircase with tar black plastic gums, clear dragonfly wings, and grooved teeth like an Aztec God ascends us to an afterworld: black, red, yellow, green, and purple carpet design is like a Jackson Pollock drip under a sixty foot cathedral ceiling with large golden Calder-like mobiles hanging at the top. The box office is to the right. The clientele is mostly forty-and-older, probably college educated, couples. We walk to an open black female cashier.

Me: Could I get two tickets to The Lonesome Circle at 7:45.

Cashier: Fourteen dollars.

The Spaghetti Bowl is the hippest restaurant in town. You pick the pasta, sauce, and extra ingredients and they make it for you. It seems most of the tables are taken but we get a good one in the corner.

People talking at various volumes and pitches echoes through the building. Maroon walls with black and gold trim are paired with dark wood floors and tables. Small bodies of ice water are stagnant in clear plastic tumblers in front of fleshy robot people. Pink, white, and brown packets of sugar are in black plastic containers. The silverware is on colored paper napkins hers is blue and mine is orange.

We fill out our orders on a card. I choose linguini in a tomato cream sauce with pork basil sausage. She chooses bowties with garlic lemon chicken in a sundried tomato sauce. I look at my legs then her. She looks at me for a moment, then I look at the people sitting behind her, and then her arm on the table.

Me: So. How long have you known Hailey?

Isabella: About two years. I've only been in the States for two and a half.

Me: Oh. Where are you from?

Isabella: Brazil.

Me: I've been close. I went to Lima to visit my aunt.

Isabella: I hear it's nice.

She thinks I am an idiot.

Me: Where are you from in Brazil?

Isabella: Sao Palo.

Me: How different is it?

Isabella: It's more exciting. There are four-story clubs and it was fun playing in the city as a kid.

More exciting than my childhood of lighting things on fire and throwing them in the canal.

Me: Why do you speak English so well?

This is a bad interview.

Isabella: Well. My mother is American and I went to an English-speaking school.

Me: Do you speak Portuguese?

Isabella: Yes.

Our food comes and we only say minor things. Her awesomeness is causing me to doubt myself.

Fear grabs me. Hot in my skull.

The mostly clear sky is starting to tint with a dusk of burnt orange and chalky pink.

Our conversation fares a little better on our walk to the movie theater. I tell her how boring my life is and about working for my uncle. She tells me about Golden Apple Tree

Road and how she put a mousetrap under her pillow to catch the tooth fairy and it snapped her father's fingers.

We have our first kiss during the previews. I used a trailer I was excited about as an excuse to kiss her. It was awkward and great.

The movie was okay. Even though the cowboy was an alcoholic the woman still loved him.

We kiss again and say goodbye.

She asks if I want to see another movie on Saturday.

We go to South Creek Court an indoor mall. It is two stories. The floor, walls, and ceiling are all different shades of beige. I fiddle with my sleeve on our way to a women's clothing store. We are in a consumer purgatory.

The store walls are arctic blue. She tries on a grey t-shirt and we make out in the changing room before a sales person demands "one person to a room." I wait outside looking at merchandise that is valueless to me.

Does Isabella like me? Maybe. Maybe she is being nice or secretly cruel.

We leave the store and walk to the movies past a 3D triangle plexiglass directory map with advertisements, a banquet hall of fast food restaurants (people dining on paper plates with plastic forks is an awkward evolution from grazing naked with a tribe in a field) a ghost piano, and a plastic playhouse for kids.

The box office looks like it could be on a spaceship: large and sleek with advanced computer technology, ticket printers in the desks, two-way metallic intercoms, and a large digital marquee with the movies and times in red lights but the employees look like early twentieth century dorks with cheesy purple vests and pleated black pants. She picks a film about an assassin in the future. The printer emits our glossy eggshell and lavender tickets with clean black print.

We take the tickets and walk to the grand lobby. The black carpet with diamond outlines of green, red, and yellow dots feels greasy under my shoes. A vacant arcade flashes in zany multicolor. The smell of nacho cheese, soda pop, hot dogs, jalapenos, popcorn, and artificial butter permeates the air. Large movie posters hang on the walls. None of this matters. I am blessed by the grace of Isabella. This graying man sitting alone in a white button-up is infinitesimal to me.

A boy with Down syndrome rips our tickets.

Ticket Taker: Theater Four is on your left.

Me: Thank you.

We sit stage right midway in the upper deck. The lights in the stairs are like runway lights. The sides of the theater are draped with rippling red velvet. I hold her hand.

During the previews we see a trailer for a picture that looks very similar to the one we are about to watch.

An assassin is escaping from an enemy building. He comes to a spacious hallway with high walls. At the other end are silver flying cube-ish robots with rapid fire guns. He sprints towards them, drawing pistols from his jacket, and shoots at them.

We held hands through the entire show. It was all I could think about. Was I holding it in the best possible way? Was my hand sweaty? Was she thinking about holding my hand?

We stand up when the credits begin to scroll. We leave the cave-like theater and walk past groups of people in the lobby to the outdoor parking lot. I hold the glass push-bar door open for her. The sky is grey. Walking past the rows saturated with cars my rubber soles shuffle on the grey pavement and gravel. She opens the locks of her grey sedan with a remote key and we get in the car. She turns to me while I am looking at the dash and out the windshield.

Isabella: Do you want to come over?

I turn to her.

Me: Yeah.

She puts the key in the ignition, turns it, shifts the automatic clutch in reverse, and backs out.

I turn the volume dial so the radio becomes audible.

Female Radio (Cartoonish): Do you want cash now? Today you can receive up to two thousand dollars cash.

I turn the station dial warping the different frequencies.

The music is difficult to describe. Drums pouncing. The guitar folds the air. Painting in vibration.

Man Singing on the Radio:
Walking covered in the neon lights,
Down on the street,
A terribly sexy night,

No one cares,
They're all full of stares,
Fashion statements go for bold,
While the young eat the old,

Cut up an eight ball,
We can't find a home,
On a mirror happiness and sadness both reflect,
The paradox of self neglect

I have to say something.

I look at the houses on trimmed green lawns with trails of smooth concrete blocks to their doors and apartment towers in the skyline. I point at a two-story white brick home.

Me: That is a nice house.

She glances out of the corner of her eye.

Isabella: Yeah.

There are so many cars so many people. What are they doing?

Her house is a blue Victorian with a painted brown porch. She parks in the empty driveway. I let her walk ahead of me. On the porch I look at her butt while she unlocks the door.

Me: Where are your parents?

Isabella: London.

She closes the door behind us and locks it. I take off my shoes using my feet.

The floors are varnished wood. All the proper space is tastefully decorated with painted ceramic vases, antique lamps, wooden tables, and photographs. A glass and bronze chandelier hangs over a long dining room table. I can see to the kitchen: white tiles, marble counter tops, and frosted glass with wood trim cabinets.

Isabella: Let's go upstairs.

I follow her to her room. She turns towards me. I grab her wrists and push her against the wall. I put my mouth against hers. Kissing. She bites my lower lip and licks my tongue. She moves me back using her left hand on my right shoulder, steps out of her sandals, and leads me into the bathroom. She opens the button of my pants, pulls down the zipper, and gives me a blowjob. I take off my shirt. I look at the top of her hair. I put my hand on her soft head. Her mouth and tongue are warm and smooth. I have her stand up and I take off her blouse, bra, and skirt. She pulls down her thong and tosses it aside. We switch places her back now to the sink. She runs her index finger like a knife down my torso. Moving my hands down her back and below her hips I lift her on the sink. I try to put my penis into her vagina but it is not moist enough so I caress and penetrate it with my left fingers. I attempt entering her slit again and my dick slides in. Grabbing the medicine cabinet mirror behind her she exhales. My hands on her thighs. We look in each other's retinas. Her hands grab my shoulders.

Isabella drives me to my apartment in silence except for directions and to say goodbye.

I stared at the windshield. Tree refractions shifting on the glass. I was like a psychotic inmate restrained by the seatbelt.

I look around my apartment in case someone broke in or something supernatural happened. My end table with a lamp, magazines, and CDs looks like it is one entity.

I am standing with nothing to do. I can feel the sweat on my body and in my clothes or it's anxiety manifested in hallucinatory perspiration. I take off my socks and pants, curl on my side, and nap in my bed.

I wake. The solar rays are fading.

I take a shower, get dressed in black mesh shorts and a white t-shirt, then sit on the couch and text Isabella.

"Hey"

I look at my phone. I sent the message four minutes ago. I put the phone on the cushion facing down. I uncross my legs and check my phone again. Sent seven minutes ago. Does she hate me?

I go into the kitchen. I turn on the oven to 325. I open the fridge and get two chicken thighs wrapped in butcher's paper. I get a square glass baking dish and a box of vegetable stock from the cabinets. Am I making a mistake caring about someone? I put the thighs in the pan, poke a few holes in with a fork, pour vegetable stock over, and season with salt, cumin, paprika, and white pepper.

I sit on the couch and check my text messages about two to three times a minute even though my phone is not on silent.

It has been about thirty-five minutes since I put the chicken in the oven. I take the dish out of the oven and check to see if the chicken is pink. Using a knife and fork I put a chicken thigh on a plate. I eat noticing the silence of my apartment. I put the dishes in the sink then wash my hands.

It is dark now.

I text Isabella again.

"Do you want to see a movie?"

I don't care about the movie. I need her affection because I am miserably alone. The agony of my loneliness is like a hell where a constant wind of a nuclear explosion slowly rips my skin; I try to scream but no one hears me.

Isabella texts me back.

"I can't maybe another time."

Maybe? Now I am doomed. I could wait here until my destiny happens. I sit on my porch and stare at telephone wires and the back of the strip mall.

*

My friend Max texts me.
"Do u want 2 hang?"
"Yeah whats up?"
"Im with david were picking you up"
"Ok"

I change to brown pants and a blue tee shirt. I brush my teeth and wipe off the foam from around my mouth with a towel. Comb my hair. I clumsily put back the toothpaste and brush in the medicine cabinet knocking over pill bottles and deodorant. I take a quick look at the mirror to confirm there is no toothpaste on my mouth and my hair is properly combed. I pour a glass of water. While I am drinking I get a phone call from Max.

Max: We're here.
Me: Okay. I'll be down.

I finish the water and set the glass on the table. I put on my shoes and get into the back driver's side seat of David's car. We all say our salutations and minor inquiries in conjunction with handshakes, low-5's, and fist bumps. I sit back and look at Max in the front seat. He is looking through his phone.

David steers the car onto the road. We meander the avenues. Windows down. Headlights illuminate the back of the car in front of us. A familiar song plays on the radio. Long grey bent-neck street lamps beam yellow on the empty sidewalks and the white line at the edge of the road. There are stores, restaurants, apartments, houses, and offices everywhere. A quasi-infinite of cars cross the intersection when the traffic light silently changes from red to green.

We anchor in a parking lot. Our doors open and slam asynchronously.

The opening of the gas station door sounds an electronic ding. A bright color spectrum of candy is meticulously displayed on a descending shelf in front of the counter. Behind the counter is a pudgy golden-brown man in a blue long sleeve buttoned corporate shirt with a worn face. His attempted stoicism does not hide his dejection.

I go look at the cooler in the back. David and Max are buying cigarettes. I have no money so I can't get nourishment.

I exit the store and lean against the car. David and Max walk out and join me by the car. They light their cigarettes hands close covering their faces in an ancient ceremony.

Two girls walk by that can't be much more than sixteen with smooth legs, gorgeous faces, and long hair. I try, unsuccessfully, ignoring them in that constant psychological erotic chess game.

David exhales followed by Max.

David: Did you hear about the shooting in Ohio?

Me: No. What happened?

David: Some guy who was fired shot his boss and two coworkers.

Me: What was the job?

David: Software company.

Max (Exhales. Making a noise like of a gust of wind): Shit. Fucked up.

Me: I heard they are raising the sales tax by two percent to help pay for the deficit and of course they plan to increase spending.

Max: I never voted for any of this.

David: Voting is an illusion of choice.

Me: No. It's not.
David: It may as well be.
They take their last drags then flick their cigarettes at the store wall. We set voyage again and roll down the automatic windows.
Me: Did you see those girls that went into the store?
David: They were so hot.
Max (Pulling his head back): Sooo hot.
Crossing defunct railroad tracks the tires rumble on rubble. We pass a lot overgrown with weeds and large abandoned buildings with boarded windows. An empty park is shaded by street lights.
I remember when I was a kid we would sneak to the local school park late at night to meet up with girls. I liked a redheaded girl named Christina the most.
I ask David to drop me off. He politely agrees.
There are more stores, more restaurants, and more office buildings on all horizons.
Me: Thanks. See you guys.
Max: See you man.
David: Bye.
I hear unseen bugs.
I open my door again. Forgetting.

I call my Uncle Bob.
Me: Can you give me an advance?
Bob: How much?
Me: Two-hundred.
Bob: Fine. Come to the office.
The bank is a small brick box with drive through ATMs and vacuum canisters shooting through clear pipes. Black mats are on the grey floors in the front entrance. On the

right are multilingual computer tellers. Inside the second doors it's colder. Free coffee and cookies are on a white doily table cloth on a fold out table. Young leather davenports. Magazines and brochures are on the table in front of the couches. More brochures sit in a tilted bookshelf-size stand next to the davenports. People in business casual sit behind desks doing vague things.

I wait beside the ribbon-poles and the island of superfluous slips. I wonder if I can get a loan to end world poverty? I promise you will see a return.

Teller: I can help you down here. I walk to the counter. Me: I want to cash this check.

I hand him the check. He examines it. He is very pale, strawberry blonde, and clean-shaven wearing a thick blue tie of shaded squares. He's probably about twenty-five.

Teller: Do you have an ID?

I grab my license from my front right pocket and hand it to him. He looks at it, types something into his computer, and hands it back to me.

Teller: Could you sign this?

He flips the check face down in front of me. I sign on the endorsement line with a pen chained to the counter. The metal grinds the hard surface when I sign and jangles when I put it back in the holder. I slide the check back to him. He flips it over and types more into the computer. He puts the check in a machine that looks like a credit card reader which automatically slides it back and forth. He takes the check out of the machiney thing and puts it somewhere in his desk.

Teller: How do you want your cash?
Me: Twenties.

He counts the money in front of me. I recount it and put it in my pocket.

Me: Thank you.

Teller: Thank you. Have a good day.

I turn around and walk out. Do people ever stay and hang out at the bank? It has heating and cooling.

The bright warm sun is uncomforting. The sinister bank has fucked with my mind. I have to reacclimate to nature.

*

I call Eddie.

Eddie: Yo.

Me: Can I get a g?

Eddie: Yeah come through.

I drive to his apartment then text him. He strolls out and gets in my car. He gives me the grass and I hand him a Hamilton.

Eddie: Hit me up again.

Me: Cool. Thanks.

He gets out.

I text Isabella.

"Do you want to go to the beach?"

"Can you pick me up?"

"Whats your address?"

"340 Maple"

"Ok Ill be there in about 40 minutes"

She in short shorts and a tank top gets in my car.

Langdon is a secluded beach in Wilmette where Sheridan Road meets Chestnut.

I park on a brick side street.

Sappy pungent cannabis crumbled into smokeable papyrus like a brown string bean. Scratch of the metal riveted wheel against flint. Snapping of the plastic tab under my thumb. The butane hisses like a dragon igniting the air with a blue orange flame.

She sucks and puffs. Exhaling the sour grey steam from our lungs.

Ashing in an archaic aluminum tray.

We fly higher than five sky scrapers.

On the road. Kentucky blue trees cinderblock sidewalk brown picket pebble driveway.

Pedestrian Frogger.

Wood ranch fence. Grassy sandy park with a centerpiece jungle gym circled by an asphalt track and humongous trees. Downward bound on a rocky trail. Tall man holding a sunbrella. Hot wife, with orange towels, and a blue cooler. Boy and girl.

The sun glares distortedly. Cotton white clouds float glacially in the air. The yellow-brown sand seems brand new. Waves are blue-green that turn into white frothy foam at their peaks and tunnels.

We sit about ten feet from the water. There are only three other people on the beach. Her large yellow towel complements her ripe lime bikini. I have a white bath towel and blue swimming trunks with tropical flowers that are out of place on a freshwater beach. Her skin is smooth and brown. She lies face up. Her eyes closed. The slopes of her legs and curve of her nether tantalize me. I get up and run into the cool water. I go under. Flowing liquid sounds fetal calm. The smooth sand is like a floor of large ribbons or miniature hills. Time seems to travel at a different speed under water. I surface pushing my feet into the wet ground. I try to run but am held to a quick march. A wave crashes at my abdomen. I turn around.

Me (Yelling): Come in.

She sits up and looks at me. The waves force me to jump and sway for my balance. She walks over to me and tries to push me backwards. I grab her wrist and pull her in. When we stand up we are two feet apart. She pulls her hair back water smashing her navel. I dive under. When I rise a blanket of water over my shoulders and back tries to keep me under. I wipe the water from my face, move towards her, and kiss her. We walk back to the shore. The waves begin to slow.

Isabella comes over.

The hinge clicks smoothly when I bolt the port. I lead to my bedroom. We French kiss. Serotonin soaks my brain.

My room is shaded like a dense forest in midday. The blazing hot sun thwarted by the curtains. Air conditioning streams through the vents.

I am still unzipping my pants by the time she is undressed. She stands demurely like an artist's model. Her nipples - perky - like pennies. I flick my boxers off my right foot. She crawls vulpinely across my bed - her knees bending in acute and obtuse angles. I kneel over her like a dog on its hinds. She lies supinely. I am insane and starving to devour her soul.

We are silent except for athletic exhalation.

We disconnect.

She says she has plans tonight and can't stay.

After she leaves I realize I am nothing without her. My hollowness can only be temporarily filled by an intoxicating faith.

I commute the elevator to do my laundry in a cold cement room with the aroma of bleach and mountain spring detergent, the mechanical splash of washing machines, tumbling heavy cloth, and metal zippers scraping the dryers.

I clean my apartment while my clothes are in the wash.

In the living room I have a 23-inch TV on an old chipped brown painted wood stand with a black video game console on a red plastic milk crate in front, a grey cord couch, a large orange and black imitation O'Keeffe floral on the wall behind the TV, and a smaller print of violets on another wall. My room has a queen-size mattress on the floor, a tall floor lamp, and my four drawer dresser. The bathroom is small and the shower has sliding glass doors. The kitchen has cheap plastic counters, grimy white tile floors, and some of the cabinet doors are missing.

I move my clothes to the dryer and continue cleaning.

I put things back in their place, throw away junk, sweep, vacuum, put dishes in the dishwasher, clean the bathroom, put back more things, throw away more stuff.

I bring down my blue plastic laundry basket and take my clothes out of the dryer.

I fold my clothes sitting on my bedroom floor.

*

Isabella texts me.
"Do you want to come to Hailey's?"
"Ya, whats the address?"

"7535 Ashland in Glenview"

"Ill let you know when Im there"

They are watching a TV show about wizards called "Charm" the type of daytime program that always ends in a cliffhanger.

I sit down on the big red leather couch next to Isabella and put my arm around her shoulders. She moves into my chest. I feel her warm heartbeat. Her soft lungs expanding and contracting.

A troll has captured one of the wizards and his friends have to find him. They end up shrinking the troll and putting him into a small wooden chest.

Me: This is pretty good.

Isabella: This show is the best.

They put on the next episode.

I lie down and Isabella moves on top me. Her ribs press comfortably into my side. I take out my cellphone and take a picture of us. It is my favorite picture ever.

A girl finds out they are wizards while they are looking for a magic jewel. The episode ends with the girl becoming their friend.

Hailey: Are you ready?

Isabella: Yeah.

Me: Ready for what?

Hailey: Bella is dying her hair.

Me: What color?

Isabella: Auburn. Here.

She shows me a laminated cardboard box with a smiling woman's profile who has reddish brown hair.

They go into the bathroom. I follow to outside the door. Isabella strips. I move into the small bathroom. Hailey opens the box and sets the contents on the counter. She has some black hairbands too. She opens the chemical packages and mixes them into a plastic squeeze bottle (like a condiment bottle). She puts on plastic gloves from the box and shakes the bottle with her thumb on the top. Bella sits on the edge of the bathtub. Hailey rubs in the dye and twists in the hairbands. Clumps of wet hair dangle over the front of Bella's shoulders. The odious chemicals burn my nostrils. I turn around and look at her reflection in the mirror. She is too good for me.

Me: Is that it?

Isabella: Now I have to wash it with this conditioner and that's it.

She takes a shower and her hair has magically changed color. She looks wonderful. We watch another episode of "Charm" where their female friend is under a spell and they have to reverse it.

I hang out with Bella and Hailey again the next night.

We are behind a mega-mart. The third wheel is to Bella's left smoking a cigarette. A post light's glaze is cast on the brick building and the concrete ledge Bella sits on. I lean against her right leg. Our shadows are tangled like our palms' digits. Heads diagonal we mash lips and fence tongues. I am a parasite of her warmth and beauty.

The dark stratosphere is speckled with a multitude of suns from inhabited galaxies away.

We go to Hailey's room. Hailey is at her computer playing music. It is a metal song with a female singer.

Me: I like this who is it?

Hailey: It's Chrissy by Sycophant. It's about a girl who killed herself on Christmas morning.

How hardcore.

In a full-length mirror I spy Bella in her brassiere. She looks back at me and smiles. She puts on her shirt and grabs a leather jacket.

Isabella: Here try this on.

Me: Is that for women?

Isabella: Yeah. But just try it on.

I take it and put it on. It is a bit small. I look at the mirror. Can't tell it's for women. I turn back to them.

Me: How does it look?

Hailey: It looks good.

Isabella: You look very sexy.

She pecks my cheek. I guess if she likes it I like it. I give it back to her. I lie down in the bed.

The song changes to a shoegazy ballad. I look at Hailey's back. She turns in her swivel chair, gets up, and climbs over me. She pulls the comforter over us. Her golden hair falls on my chest. We embrace with our mouths. She puts her hand on my cock and I kiss her again. She opens the button of my pants. Her hand mangled in my boxers rubs my veins until they fill with blood. Will Isabella enjoy sharing me? Maybe she is fine with it. She hasn't said anything or tried to stop it. Gripping. Stroking. She straddles my left leg with her bottom half. She breathes into my neck. I make the effort to stop her and close my pants. I move the cover.

Isabella is sitting in front of Hailey's computer. She turns to us. Her eyes look like they are saturated with tears. Am I imagining that? She does not cry. She is not saying anything. That must mean she does not care. Is this denial? I sit on the edge of the bed, pull her over, and kiss her. It's fine but I know it is not. Her world has darkened and a knife has been stabbed into her chest. Hopefully it will be okay. How selfish of me. How human.

Isabella leaves before me and I say goodbye to Hailey. I feel like shit as I drive home.

Light of the afternoon shines through my windows. I am on the couch. It is quiet. School must have ended. Large buses are bumping down the streets. Traffic appears. Children run and yell. I text Isabella
"What are you doing?"
"Don't talk to me."
"But I love you"
She does not text me back.

*

I had a dream that I was starving and thirsty. I walked to the end of the Earth and everyone refused to feed me or give me water.

I call my grandfather Richard.
Richard: Hey Alex. How's it going?
Me: Uhh. All right. I was wondering if I could come to the T.C. for a while.
Richard: Sure. We would love to have you. I could pick you up on Friday and bring you back Sunday if that is all right?
Me: All right.
Richard: See you buddy.
Me: Thanks. Bye.
Richard: Goodbye.

I get a text from Vincent.
"What are you doing? I'm at the airport"

I did not know he was coming into town.
"Nothing"
"I'm coming to pick you up"
"Okay"

Vincent is one of my oldest friends. We know each other from the school bus. He was a new kid in town when I first met him. He wore his hat backwards and listened to the latest rap on his Walkman. Now he's into calfskin wallets and Ecuadorian lounge singers from the sixties. He is in the movie business. He gets producers to place certain products in their films.

I change my clothes and sit on the couch for a while before becoming anxious and putting in a video game. After twenty minutes of slaughtering aliens Vincent calls me.

Vincent: Yo.
Me: Yo.
Vincent: Yeah. I'm here.
Me: Okay.
Vincent: Okay.

He is in a European luxury car blasting Kung Fu themed rap.

Rapper:
Karate kicking for kilometers
He turns down the volume.
Vincent: We're going to a party.
Me: Whose?
Vincent: A girl I know.
Me: How do you know her?
Vincent: She wants to be an actress.
He starts driving.
Me: Where is it?
Vincent: Buffalo Grove.

Me: So. Why are you back?

Vincent: Visiting the family. How are you?

Me: I'm all right. I was hanging out with this girl but she hates me now.

Vincent: That sucks.

Me: What's up with you?

Vincent: Nothing really. I went to the Bahamas a few weeks ago.

Me: How was that?

Vincent: Good. I just stayed on the beach and got a tan.

I turn up the volume. We both have changed since we were younger and don't know how to handle it.

We arrive at the house. The lights are on but it does not look like a party is happening. Vincent parks on the street. He texts Julia then we walk to the door. It is dark but the glow of the neighborhood illuminates the landscape. My legs move in front of each other. It seems like all my existence is walking to this door.

She opens the front door. We are introduced. They walk away and disappear.

On the kitchen counter are liquor bottles and soda. I pour myself a rum and cola. It bubbles like a witch's cauldron.

Music seeps from the basement like a hypnotic symphony of cough syrup, prescription pills, and purple Kush spilled over turntables.

I saunter down the stairs with an emphasized landing on my heels when I hit a step. I reach the bottom of the stairs and turn my head surveying the room like I am going to know someone. It could be a scene in a nature documentary about humans.

There are about sixteen people in the basement. I hear the gurgle and clearing of a bong then see the smoke billow from behind someone's head who is sitting in a metal folding chair. A group of surrounding people fiend for some indica and beyond them is a pool table converted to a beer pong table by a piece of plywood. At the table a kid with bifocals plays against a large muscular dude - arms bent like taking jump shots. They both miss. The kid with glasses dips the ball in a cup of water.

I sit on the open couch and stretch my arms on the backrest. Observing the panorama. The energy is pulsating in a chaotic twisting circular motion or I imagine it to be. A round white table lamp with a brown cloth shade is dimly beaming.

Rapper:
I'm a promiscuous epicurean,
Rebel like a Syrian,
I shop at Nordstrom's,
And drink rum,
Rhymes intricate like needle points of military engagements or soirées in basements

I go upstairs. There are some people in the backyard. I explore the residence. White upholstered couches are on wood floors in the living room. I go to the second level and into the first room on the left. A carpeted office with a large desk and computer. Behind are unadorned shelves. A treadmill is folded up in the corner.

I go back into the hall and hear a door open down the way. Julia sticks her head out of the doorway.

Julia: What are you doing?

Me: Just looking around.

Vincent comes into the doorway. The look of sex is in their eyes.

Vincent: I'll find you before I leave or let me know if you get a ride with someone else.

Me: Yeah. I will.

He closes the door and I go back downstairs. I walk through the kitchen to the sliding door and step outside. A group of people stand semi-circled beyond the porch light. A few people look towards me and return to their conversation.

Girl 1: So I asked to return it. She was such a bitch. She gave me this look and said they only give store credit. So I told her to get the manager and she said the same thing. So I just got it in a different color.

Girl 2: That happened to me at Brandy's and I was like so pissed.

Back inside. I pour myself another drink. I see a cute girl on the couch. I walk over and sit down next to her.

Me: Hey. I'm Alex.

I put out my hand for her to shake. She lightly squeezes it.

Girl: Hey.

Me: What's your name?

Girl: Taylor.

Me: Well. Do you like this party?

Taylor: Uhh. It's okay.

Me: Do you like the music?

Taylor: Yeah. It's fine.

Me: How do you feel about the war in Iraq?

Taylor: I don't know.

Me: Okay. Well. Nice to meet you.

Back to the basement. I sit on the couch and try to listen to the music as if there is not a party happening.

I go to the pool table.

Me: Can I play winner?
Guy: You can play next winner.
Me: Okay.
I go back to the sofa and stare at the floor and wall.
Guy: Hey. It's your turn.
Me: Okay.

I set up the red cups in the regulation pyramid shape, fill them with three beers, and throw the empty cans in a white trash bag tied on a doorknob.

I win but let someone take my spot.

In the kitchen two bags of chips are open next to a clear plastic tray with cookie crumbs in it. I take one potato chip and eat it. Then about four more and then two or three more. With the dwindling rum I pour another drink. Vincent and Julia come down.

Vincent: Ready to go?
Me: Yeah.

I chug my drink and put the cup in the trash.

Me: It was nice to meet you.
Julia: Yeah. You too.

Vincent parks in front of my apartment building. He got a joint from Julia. We hotbox his rental. We get into a pedantic discussion as always when we're high.

Me: Either God exists or God does not exist. That brings me to the question of what is spontaneous reality and how would it compare to a created reality? Because if God wanted he could have made the grass red.

Vincent: You can't question empirical data because it is only observation not a conclusion. Whatever exists is natural whether God created it or not.

The music has stopped.

Me: Nature follows rules. One of the few arguments for God is: Things have no rules so God could exist. Probably reality exists because it has to and therefore we are a product of chance. What I don't understand is how can all these religious people know they are correct? Their beliefs contradict each other so they can't all be true.

Vincent: That's like Baha'i-esque.

Me: Yeah. Baha'i. Jesus, Mohamad, Krishna were all Baha'i.

Vincent: Well. The atheists are right anyway.

Me: I don't know about that.

Vincent: Prove there is an all-powerful creator.

Me: You can't prove it's not true.

Vincent: Yeah. The Big Bang created the universe.

Me: That is a logical flaw. You can't say you don't think God created the universe but the Big Bang did. I could say the universe was brewed in a teapot. Scientists are convinced the Big Bang created the universe as the religious are convinced God did it.

Vincent: Maybe logic is wrong. I should become an alogicist. I don't believe in formal logic.

Me: Socrates was a myth created to make people anti capital punishment.

Vincent: Yeah. Definitely.

He takes the last hit of the joint and throws it out the window.

Vincent: Okay. Well. I'm going to go. Hopefully we can hang out again before I leave.

Me: I'm going to my grandparents' tomorrow.

Vincent: Sucks. Well try to come to L.A. sometime.

Me: I will.

I get out of the car.

I put on a CD and sprawl on my carpet. I just want to lie here on the carpet, semi-comatose, forever.

*

My grandfather calls me and says he is outside my apartment. I throw some clothes in a gym bag.

The Tri Cities are four cities dissected by a river valley. New cul-de-sacs are constructed like labyrinths. Victorian manors and stone mansions, some abandoned and dilapidating, are on the hills.
We weave through a ravine of tall skinny trees, past secluded estates, and down a slope. We pull up behind a rusted blue pickup truck, next to a cemetery, before crossing a green steel trapezoidal bridge stretching over the faded denim river. A pink casino is docked on the riverbank. We tow up the other hill and turn onto his street. A famous gangster once lived on his block (before he ever lived there) in what's now a collapsing castle.
Across the street from the bootlegging building is his house a two story brownstone with a bit of ivy. A car lot that could fit about six cars holds their two. Where the lot meets the grass of the backyard is a boxed garden, about six by twelve feet, with tomatoes, cucumbers, jalapenos, cilantro, and a few rotating variables. There is also a flower garden against the side of the house with tulips and geraniums. To the right of the carport is an old brown barn used for storage and to the right of that is a patio where summer parties and Labor Day were once held. Weeds blossom in the dirt spaces between old bricks.
We go through the back screen door.

Me: Hello.
Diane: Hey Alex. It's good to see you.
She gives me a hug.
Me: Yeah. It's good to see you too.
Diane: How have you been?
Me: I've been okay nothing new.
Richard puts my bag in my uncle's old room.
Richard: So. What do you want for dinner?
Me: Pizza.
Richard: What type?
Me: Canadian bacon and sauerkraut.

The most authentic local cuisine other than corn and pork chops.

Richard: Diane doesn't like Canadian bacon and sauerkraut. Can we get taco pizza too?

Too? That is better.

Me: Yeah. Sounds good.
Richard: Where do you want to get it from?
Me: Harry's.
Richard: Okay. I'll call it in and go pick it up.
Me: Okay.
He calls the pizza place.
Richard: They said only fifteen minutes. I'll go get it now.
I ask to go with but he wants to go alone.
I go to the living room and turn on the local news.

The weather and the sports scores are the worst parts of the news and they take up about twenty percent of the broadcast. If I wanted to know either of them I would look them up on the internet or in the newspaper.

He returns with the pies. Two circles in brown cardboard boxes. We eat the slices on white paper plates. Diane uses a fork and knife. They taste spectacular, almost seem healthy.

After clearing the table we play a game of cards. The ancient symbols secret in my hands. I win three of the four games. Diane wins the other.

We watch a movie about a doctor who has to save her daughter from a mysterious disease.

They go upstairs. I flip through the channels.

I think about Bella for a second then my euphoria turns into regret and self-hatred.

My uncle's room smells faintly of old tobacco.

Coffee grinding. I put on my pants and socks, go to the bathroom, then sit down at the breakfast table.

Richard: Do you want any eggs?

Me: No thanks. Do you have any bagels and cream cheese?

Richard: Yes. The bagels are in the cupboard and cream cheese is in fridge.

I put a bagel in the toaster and then spread on cream cheese.

We watch the national news on a small TV next to the breakfast nook in the kitchen.

News Anchor: The United States government is issuing an apology to the people of Kandahar for accidentally killing civilians in a mission targeting combatants in the area. Recently the region has been active with terrorists.

They have two guests "weigh in."

I can't stand listening to watered-down middle-of-the-road fluff for too long so I go to the computer and check my email. Nothing. I text my cousin Josh.

"Im in town. What are you doing?"

I go into the living room and sit on the couch. Richard comes in and turns on the TV.

"Nothing do you want to come over"

Me: Will you drop me off at Josh's?

Richard: Sure. Let me get ready.

I text Josh.

"Yeah, grandpa is dropping me off"

Josh has been somewhat estranged from the family for his many arrests and the copious amount of drugs he does. He's only been convicted once though.

I knock on his door. He opens it ajar then lets me in.

Me: Hey.

Josh: Hey.

I walk in and sit on the couch. He locks the door behind me. His clothes are tossed on chairs and the floor, and there are plates, cups, forks, spoons, knives, pizza boxes strewn around. He sits down packing a bowl.

Smoke begins to accumulate. Then the fear sets in. My body is tense. Something bad is going to happen. A bomb is going to explode. I am going to be wrongfully imprisoned. There is nothing I can do so I have to ignore it.

Josh: Do you think politicians ever acknowledge the truth about making decisions based on the fiscal benefits for the rich?

Me: Do you mean publicly? Probably not.

Josh: No. I mean to their aides and stuff.

Me: I don't know. Maybe some of them do.

Josh: There has to be politicians out there that are so crazy they don't even think about what they're doing and choose their policies based on what seems like the best idea for them at the moment.

Me: Many people are probably like that.

We discuss businesses we will never start, for a while, because we don't have enough money.

He offers me some china white. I decline. He pours half of a gram on a CD and snorts it all.

Richard texts me that Angela Josh's mother is coming to dinner tonight and wanted to know if I would come back. I said I would.

Richard picks me up an hour later. I try to be less high.
Me: What's up with Angela and Martin?
Richard: They just got back tonight from a cruise in Florida. Martin's mother just died.
Me: Oh. where did they go?
I'm not good with others' grief.
Richard: They went to Puerto Rico and the Bahamas.
Me: What are we eating?
Richard: Steak, potatoes, and asparagus.
Me: Okay.

He parks in the driveway. I go to the living room and watch TV as they cook dinner.

I watch a primetime show about people competing to become racecar drivers. There is a shouting-fight in their communal house because someone stole another guy's pop. A guy with knuckle tattoos loses an off-road race. They take away his keys. Meaning he is gone from the program.

I go to the kitchen. Richard is bringing the steaks off the grill and Diane takes the asparagus out of the oven.

Headlights strike through the kitchen window as a car turns into the driveway. Angela, her husband Martin, and their kids Emma and Ryan walk into the kitchen.

Angela: Hey. You guys the kids are sick.
They look sick and tired. Ryan coughs.

Diane: Oh no! What happened?

Angela: I think it is just a cold. They got it on the last day of the cruise.

Martin: Hey. Alex.

We shake hands.

Martin: How's it going?

Me: Good. How are you?

Martin: Fine. We just got back from a cruise.

Me: Yeah. I heard. How was it?

Martin: Yeah. It was good the kids really liked it.

Richard: Well. The food is ready if you guys are ready to eat. Alex put their coats in your room.

Me: Okay.

I take their coats and put them on the bed.

Angela: I got the kids fast food so I don't think they're going to eat.

Richard: That's all right. Hopefully you guys are hungry.

Martin: The food looks good Richard.

Richard: Thank you.

Diane and Richard bring all the food into the dining room and set it down.

The steak is good but there needs to be some tomatoes.

Richard (Coughing): The potatoes.

He tries to take a sip of water but it comes back up. Was he mocking the kids for being sick? It's not funny. Gasping he gets out of his chair. It is clear now that he is choking. Diane follows him into the kitchen. Will he make it? The kids ask what's happening. Angela and I get up and go to the kitchen. Standing near the sink he is breathing like a hippo through a tiny straw.

Diane: Something is stuck in his throat.

He goes into the bathroom trying to recover. Diane comforts him in the bathroom. After Diane calls her sister Thelma, whose husband Walton sometimes has similar issues with the obstruction of the esophagus, she decides he needs to go to the ER. Angela offers to massage the area but Diane dismisses it like it is savage witchcraft. After Angela tries to rub the affected spot with no relief Diane takes him to the ER.

Martin and I continue to eat as if nothing has happened. We discuss the cruise and our hopes of the Bears reaching the playoffs.

When Richard gets back he looks very sedated and he softly says he can't drive tomorrow. So I look for a bus ticket.

Diane drops me at the station. The bus is almost full. I see a girl in back by herself.

Me: Can I sit there?

She moves her 24-oz. bottle of brown pop and cheese chips from the seat and I sit down.

She was from a small town. I can tell by her dirty white tennis shoes, worn grey sweatpants, and pink and yellow sweatshirt.

Lying on her side she pushes her knees into my legs. I try giving her more room but her knees continue to press against me. Is that an engagement ring on her finger? I try to move my legs again but it's no use resisting. I will have to enjoy this moment of public bus petting.

She gets off at the side of the road about two hours from the city.

We pass one continuous field before we arrive downtown.

I grab my bag, walk down the aisle, and step off the bus. I walk through the bus station and head to the train.

Cellphone plans include smiles. Vacation in Afghanistan. We emerge from underground. People hold the overhead railings. People civilly transfer lines on the platform. I get on the Yellow Line and depart at the last stop.

*

I dial my friend Ollie.
Ollie: Yo.
Me: Yo. Do you want to go to Winners?
Winners is a pool bar I kind of hate but it is the only bar Ollie goes to because he can walk to it and they will serve him without his ID which is often lost.
Ollie: Yeah. I'll be there in twenty minutes.
Me: Okay. Bye.
Ollie: Peace.
I'm walking by a window and see Ollie at the side end of the bar. He sits at the bar because he likes a waitress named Kat.

I open the front door and walk past the men with grey beards waiting to return to work. When did they turn forty and sad? Temporarily they will forget immersed in ethanol, that tastiest cold gold, later to sober and recognize the silver paperweight on a shelf in their house.

Ollie has two beers in front of him. I sit down next to him.
Ollie (Grabbing a beer): Here. I got you this.
Me: Thank you.
Pool balls broken tap like rainfall and disperse across the bright blue felt like the canvas of a Kandinsky. The players circle the table with predatory strides.

Me: Do you want to play pool?
Ollie: No. Let's just sit here.
Me: Come on.
I get the bartender's attention.
Me: Could I get a cue ball?
She gets one from below the counter and hands it to me. Ollie goes to the pool table closest to the bar. I put my beer on a table near Ollie.

Next to the rigged arcade game (you are a man who has to fly past buildings to collect coins – it's free but you can never win or score any points) is the change machine.

I feed the change machine a dollar and quarters slide out. I grab them and walk back to the table. With the four coins standing in the metal slots I push the lever in. The balls roll out and I rack them. Ollie chalks a cue and breaks. None go in. I make a stripe.

Ollie: Have you heard the new Big Juicy song?
Me: No. Is it good?
I follow the white ball.
Ollie: Yeah man. All Big Juicy songs are good.
I make another ball then miss.
Ollie: He's on a new record label and Evil Storm does the production.
Me: Have you heard Darien Harris?
Ollie: No. But I've heard of him.
Me: He is amazing. It is some of my favorite rap I have ever heard. He is so honest one of his songs almost made me cry.
Ollie: I'll have to listen to him.

Twisted neon lights above heads. The smashing stones are louder than the rock music playing.

Ollie wins with the eight ball in a corner pocket.

A brunette woman is sitting at the bar. I imagine fucking her. My tongue moving up her ribs. I grab her hair pulling back. Our skin pressed against each other's. A thin sheet over our bodies protecting against the cold air.

I look back at Ollie.

Me: Do you want to hang out with Lauren and Michael?

Ollie: Yeah. Should I call them?

Me: Sure.

Ollie calls them.

Ollie: Lauren is going to pick up Michael and then they're coming.

Ollie gets a text and I change another dollar. I return to the table.

Ollie: Becky is coming.

Me: No! Why did you do that?

Ollie: She wanted to come so I invited her.

Me: Ahh! This is so bad!

I hate Becky. She is lazy and selfish. If she does not like something she disagrees with it. For example if she did not like swimming then no one should ever swim. Once I got off the bus two blocks too far when she was picking me up and she was angry at me for making a mistake. She once asked to bang me. I said "no thanks." She is obsessed with a guy I went to high school with John or as she calls him "Johnny."

We sit down at a table - in the kind of chairs where your feet don't touch the ground.

Oh fuck. There they are. All of them are silent. Lauren is grinning with the enjoyment of a spectator anticipating our hatred. Becky is nervously smiling trying not to look at me but she is. Michael is oblivious to our animosity.

Becky: Hey Alex.

Me: Hey.

Lauren: So. What are you guys up to?

Me: Just drinking and playing pool. Is there anything to do?

Lauren: Not that I know of. I thought maybe we could go to a club.

Me: Which club?

Lauren: Bright Lights.

Ollie: Why can't we just stay here?

Becky: Ollie. Come on. We're going to the club.

Ollie: All right. All right. We'll go to the club.

Michael: Then we're going to the spaceship with cats.

Becky forcefully chuckles.

Becky: What are you talking about Michael?

Michael: We're going on a spaceship after.

Becky: Okay Michael.

Lauren: Ollie. Do you have your ID?

Ollie: Yeah.

We all start to leave. I grab the door and walk out followed by everyone else.

Me: Shotgun.

Becky: No. I get shotgun.

Me: I just said it.

Becky: But I get shotgun. I'm a girl.

Me: That's not how it works.

Becky: Alex. Give me shotgun!

I open the door and start to get in.

Becky: Alex. I'm not going to get in unless I get shotgun.

I would be fine with leaving her but I know Lauren won't do that.

Me: Fine. Cry if you don't get what you want.

I get out and shut the door behind me. I get in the back and realize the hypocrisy of my statement.

Lauren gets in the driver's seat of her SUV.

Lauren: Who wants to play music?

Me: Not Becky.

Michael: Yeah. Not Becky.

Michael and Ollie agree with my opinion that Becky has the worst taste in music. She likes Electro Pop. And her choices are bad. It sounds like goats being strangled over Dixieland jazz played by synthesized bagpipes.

Michael sits in the middle. He is the biggest. His hairy brown legs stick out of his shorts and are bumping my legs.

Ollie: Do you have "Elbow a Thug" or "Playa Playa?"

Me: Yeah.

Lauren: Do you have "Gangsta Elbows?"

Ollie: It's "Elbow a Thug."

Becky: Do you have "I'm a Gangsta Gangsta?"

Lauren: I don't have any rap. I have some Albanian singing.

Michael: Here. Give me the cord.

He plays a folk singer from the seventies playing a Spanish guitar.

Folk Singer:

I am broken and no one cares

Becky: Do we have to listen to this?

Michael: Come on. This is good!

Ollie: Yes. We have to.

With the tinted windows, building lights, and street lamps it is a few tones darker inside the car than out.

We park at a meter.

Would you save more money if you chose not to pay the meter and occasionally got a ticket? Is there a limit on how many parking tickets you can get? It is outrageous how ignorant I am as a citizen of my country's laws.

Buzzed people are smoking outside of the entrance. Our IDs to the bouncer. Enter the club.

Flashing lights. Guys with their collars popped, fake tans, gelled hair, and wraparound arm tattoos. Girls with lower back tattoos in tube tops and miniskirts.

We sit down on a bench attached to the wall.

Michael: This music is so bad.

The crowd dancing and grinding heats the discotheque.

I like this song. Never mind. I guess it's a mash-up.

Me: Does someone want to dance?

They look at me from their seats.

Lauren: No. I just want to dance here.

She flails her arms.

Me: Come on. You guys are no fun.

I dance for the thirty seconds of the song I like then sit back down.

A breeze from a fan refreshes me.

A girl does some twerking with her hands on the wall. I think I am the only one that watches. Her two friends look serious standing with their arms folded.

Michael: I'm getting a headache.

Ollie looks like he is enjoying himself but he is just sitting staring at the wall across the floor. I try dancing again in a general area but I guess I am not cool enough to be someone's partner so I sit down for the night unless someone wants to ask me to dance.

Michael left. Ollie and I go look for him. He is standing near the curb.

Me: Why are you out here?

Michael: The music is terrible.

Ollie: It's not that bad.
Me: I'm sure you can convince Lauren to go.

*

I enter the ice cream parlor through a glass pull door - chilly from air conditioning - grey tile floor with red and white striped walls - square tables with black metal legs. A short blonde girl in a white polo and black baseball cap with a round red face is behind the counter wielding a silver ice cream scoop. She seems nice. I step to the buffet and look through the tilted glass at the multicolored frozen milk flavors in round cardboard tubs.

Ice cream vendor: How may I help you?
Me: Could I get the caramel sea salt pecan in a waffle cone?

She puts on disposable gloves, and grabs a waffle cone from a cumbersome glass box beside the ice cream selections, walks to the middle of the bar, leans over the tub and sculpts an orb. After handing me the edible melting sculpture, she presses the order onto a screen, and gives me change.

There are people at the tables outside the shop. I don't want to be near them. I turn the corner and walk down a block mostly covered by the shade of trees. An older portly Asian woman in a white and blue dress is watering her garden with a spray-nozzle hose. A bird lands on her lawn and flies away quickly.

I rotate the cone in my hand and lap the dripping ice cream. The sunlight and the shade are mixed with the wind. A metal wind chime dings though things seem still. What is it like from across the street or backwards? Is that possible?

I ride my bike to the forest preserve and sit down, in a coved meadow, next to my capsized bike. Some tall wheat-like grasses bounce and flap in the wind. Lone birds fly near the tree tops.

The shadows bend like a sun dial.

I pick up my bike and walk it back to the path. What is there to do? I ride into town. Streetlights, commercial pharmacies, law offices, and Japanese restaurants stretch on for blocks. No one else is on the sidewalk. Hundreds of cars drive by. I turn down into the residential area and ride down a street with no sidewalk.

I bike in circles at a school. Cracks are in the asphalt like varicose veins. I grasp my fingers through a green plastic coated chain fence and balance myself on my bike.

As I am riding by a large gas station on a corner close to my house a car pulls up next to me going the other direction.

Teenage front seat passenger: Fuck you asshole!

I turn back to look at them and they speed away. I don't think I know them. How did they know I am an asshole?

I pass a woman in a burka carrying a little boy.

Across the street at the park three men are playing a game of probably twenty-one on the green clay basketball court.

Some people's lights are on in my building. I get off my bike, walk it through the lobby, and put it in my storage locker.

*

I wake up in a sweaty heat. I am sick. I roll my head and turn my body around in the bed. I toss off the hot blanket and go to the bathroom. I get back in bed and pull a sheet over me. I twist my head around the pillow futilely.

Tentacles pull me into a realm of the eternal.

A boat fights forward against the waves on a rainy night. Murky reflections on a night's window.

Water is flooding past my head not following traditional gravity.

A house saturated with trapped sweltering people.

I stand in a long hall. Isabella appears about thirty feet away. I go closer and she vanishes. I can't let her disappear. All three doors I try to open are locked. I find one that is open. A balcony in a city. Walking below metal robots patrol the streets. Their waists above two-story houses. I turn around open the door and enter a large room. A long line of people are in chairs with TV screens in front of their faces and speakers beside their ears. Feeding tubes and waste containers are attached to their chairs. I go through another door. It leads to more doors. I open one to a prop-like-room with random objects tossed in a jumble like a tennis racket and a salmon. I can't find her anywhere.

The sky is whited out. An eye is watching me. I am covered in clear slime but can't feel it.

There is a lone man holding a chisel who is carving the letter "n" in "dean" on a large marble slab.

I am in a dark room on a bed paralyzed. Where is Isabella? A doctor starts giving me injections in my arm. I need Isabella. He starts to surgically open my chest. I move my hand towards his mask and pull it off. It is me. The room is mine.

*

Bella. Bella. Isabella. Isabella. Isabella. I am infested by thoughts and feelings for her. I remember exactly how she kisses and I can feel it sometimes. I think of holding her in my arms pressed against my chest. Does she care about me at all? I wonder all the time. I would sacrifice almost anything to go back in time to change things. I would be a wonderful person to her if I could. I am such a fool. I would crawl and beg to be back with her but then I would probably leave her if she took me back. She probably does not miss me and does not care about my pain and it hurts so much. There are other girls but Isabella is the only one I want to be with right now. A heaviness weighs over me even when I try to suppress thoughts of her. I want to cry but that would mean I am past her and I don't want to let go. All I can do is lie down and try to hide from myself.

*

Amanda calls me.
Amanda: Do you want to hang out?
Me: What happened to your boyfriend?
Amanda: We broke up.
Me: Oh. So. Do you want to go to dinner?
Amanda: Yeah.
Me: Okay. I'll pick you up.
We go to Red Zebra. The host seats us at a table in the back. He is also a server. He brings us water with seemingly intentional silence.

Should I tell her about Bella? It's not important to her and I don't want to talk about it.

We discuss the menu. She decides to have the lamb with white wine and I get the duck with a red. An older waiter memorizes our order. A large group of businessmen are at a long table drinking and laughing.

Me (Pointing toward the group): They look like they are in Citizen Kane.

She looks at them.

Amanda: Oh.

The host returns. A cylinder light hanging above our table shines on his face. He bows like a matador with grace in his acquaintance of death and pours the wine. The glass is cold.

I look at a Henri Rousseau-like picture of flowers in a vase. The petals wilt and drip into blood. The businessmen take the trays, walk around, and serve the waiters. A woman in high heels is standing by the bar. Stitched into the back of her right ankle is black thread. A man in his late fifties, sitting with, probably, his wife, is served a tart with a spiral carved on its top hazel crust. It is turned over. Inside are strawberries and raspberries glistening like exotic gems.

The waiter brings our food.

My duck is very good. She says she likes her lamb.

I park in front of her apartment.

I unzip my pants. Her hair rests on my lap. I finish quickly.

She opens the door. I turn to her.

Me: Bye.

She looks back at me.

Amanda: Bye.

She gets out and shuts the door.

The stars are faint in the sky.

Here is my personal project:

www.helpfindmytruelove.com

To write: xavierjayrichards@aol.com

Made in United States
Cleveland, OH
29 October 2025